For Ma & Pa

ERROLL
A JONATHAN CAPE BOOK 978 0 224 07093 5

Published in Great Britain by Jonathan Cape,
an imprint of Random House Children's Books
A Random House Group Company

This edition published 2009

1 3 5 7 9 10 8 6 4 2

RANDOM HOUSE CHILDREN'S BOOKS
61–63 Uxbridge Road, London W5 5SA

www.kidsatrandomhouse.co.uk
www.rbooks.co.uk

Addresses for companies within The Random House Group Limited
can be found at: www.randomhouse.co.uk/offices.htm

THE RANDOM HOUSE GROUP
Limited Reg. No. 954009

A CIP catalogue record for
this book is available
from the British Library.

Printed in Malaysia

The nicest Nutti Nutts!

JONATHAN CAPE • LONDON

ERROLL

by
Hannah Shaw

One day, Bob found a squirrel in his packet of nuts.

"**Crikes!**" yelled Bob.

"*Yikes!*" squeaked the squirrel.

Bob was sure that squirrels didn't usually talk, so this one must be rather *special*.

"I'm Bob," said Bob eagerly. **"What's your name?"**

"I'm Erroll," replied the squirrel with a t o o t h y grin.

Bob could only imagine how Erroll had got inside the packet of nuts in the **first place . . .**

"You must be **hungry** **after all that,**" said Bob.

So he made Erroll a peanut-butter sandwich. And another . . . and another . . .

"**I like peanut butter, too,**" said Bob politely.

Erroll **stuffed** his face, spraying crumbs everywhere.

Soon he was covered from **head to toe** in peanut butter.

"You need a bath!" said Bob.
But Erroll didn't seem to like water.

"It's got bubbles," said Bob.
But Erroll didn't seem
to like bubbles, either.

In the end, Bob tried cleaning Erroll
with his mum's toothbrush . . .

It took a **very** long time to catch Erroll after that . . .

Finally, Bob cornered him.

A trail of

dirty

paw

prints

led him all the way to the top
of Mum's favourite curtains,
where Erroll was swinging

dangerously.

"If you like climbing so much, there's a big tree in our garden," said Bob, hoping Erroll would make less mess outside.

Erroll scrambled up the tree as quick as a flash. He sat at the top waiting for Bob.

"It's a very long way down," said Bob, trying not to sound scared.

"Oh no, I'm stuck," he wailed a few moments later.

Luckily, Erroll was there
to help him climb down safely.

Back on the ground,
Bob could hear his mum shouting.
She sounded very cross.

"**Hallo,**" said Erroll.

"Aggghhhh!"

cried Bob's mum.

Bob told his mum everything.

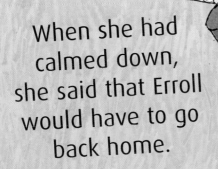

When she had calmed down, she said that Erroll would have to go back home.

"Not back in the packet!" said Bob in dismay.

"No, back to the woods!" said his mum.

Bob was sad that Erroll
was going home,
even if he had got him
into lots of trouble.

He made Erroll a
triple-mega
peanut-butter
sandwich
as a goodbye
present.

"**Goodbye, Erroll,**" said Bob.
And when his mum wasn't looking,
he whispered,
"Come back
and visit
any time!"

"Bye-bye, Bob," said Erroll.

Erroll's friends were extremely pleased to see him again.

He told them all about his adventures with his new friend Bob.

Nut-Store

The next day, Bob had **muesli** for breakfast . . .